Rumblewick's ~~My~~ Diary

My Unwilling Witch Goes to Ballet School

Hiawyn Oram • Sarah Warburton

LITTLE, BROWN AND COMPANY
Books for Young Readers
New York   Boston

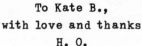

To Kate B.,
with love and thanks
H. O.

For Lucy
S. W.

Text copyright © 2007 by Hiawyn Oram
Illustrations copyright © 2007 by Sarah Warburton

Little, Brown Books for Young Readers

Hachette Book Group
237 Park Avenue, New York, NY 10017
Visit our Web site at www.lb-kids.com

Little, Brown Books for Young Readers is a division of Hachette Book Group,
Inc. The Little, Brown name and logo are trademarks of Hachette Book Group, Inc.

First U.S. Edition: May 2009
First published in Great Britain in 2007 by Orchard Books

Library of Congress Cataloging-in-Publication Data

Oram, Hiawyn.
My unwilling witch goes to ballet school / by Hiawyn Oram ; illustrated by Sarah
Warburton. —1st U.S. ed.
p. cm. — (Rumblewick's diary ; #1)
Summary: Rumblewick, a Highly Qualified Witch's Cat, records in his diary all the problems
he has when his reluctant young witch decides she would rather go to ballet school on the
Other Side than engage in proper witch behavior.
ISBN 978-0-316-03472-2
[1. Witches—Fiction. 2. Cats—Fiction. 3. Ballet dancing—Fiction. 4. Diaries—Fiction. 5.
Humorous stories.] I. Warburton, Sarah, ill. II. Title.
PZ7.0624Mr 2009
[Fic]—dc22
2009000201

10 9 8 7 6 5 4 3 2 1

RRD-C

Printed in the United States of America

CONTRACT OF SERVICE

between
WITCH HAGATHA AGATHA, Haggy Aggy for short, HA for shortest
of Thirteen Chimneys, Wizton-under-Wold

&

the Witch's Familiar,
RUMBLEWICK SPELLWACKER MORTIMER B, RB for short

It is hereby agreed that, come
FIRE, Brimstone, CAULDRONS overflowing,
or ALIEN WIZARDS invading,
for the NEXT SEVEN YEARS
RB will serve HA,
obey her EVERY WHIM AND WORD and at all times assist her
in the ways of being a true and proper WITCH.

PAYMENT for services will be:
* a log basket to sleep in   * unlimited slime buns for breakfast
* free use of HA's broomsticks (outside of peak brooming hours)
* and a cracked mirror for luck.

PENALTY for failing in his duties will be decided on the whim of
THE HAGS on HIGH.

SIGNED AND SEALED
this New Moon Day, 22nd of Remember

Haggy Aggy
....
Witch Hagatha Agatha

Rumblewick
....
Rumblewick Spellwacker Mortimer B

Trixie Fiddlestick
....
And witnessed by the High Hag, Trixie Fiddlestick

A SHORT HISTORY
OF HOW YOU COME TO BE READING MY
VERY PRIVATE DIARIES

In a snail shell, they were STOLEN. Oh yes, no less. My witch, Haggy Aggy (HA for short), sneaked into my log basket and helped herself.

According to her, this is what happened:

On one of her many shopping trips to Your Side she met a Book Wiz. (I am told you call them publishers, though Wiz seems more fitting as they make books appear, as if by magic, every day of the week.)

Anyway, this Book Wiz/publisher wanted HA to write an account of HER life as a witch here on Our Side. Of course, HA wasn't willing to do that. Being the most unwilling witch in witchdom, she is far too busy shopping, watching TV, not cackling, being anything BUT a witch, and getting me into trouble with the High Hags* as a result.

The Book Wiz begged on her knees (apparently) and offered HA a life's supply of shoes if she came up with something. So HA did. She came up with THIS — MY DIARIES. ALL OF THEM!!!!

Of course, when I wrote the diaries, I was not expecting anyone to read them. Let alone Othersiders like you. But as you are, here is a word to the wise about how things work between us:

* The High Hags run everything around here. They RULE.

1. We are here on THIS SIDE and you are there on the OTHER SIDE.

2. Between us is the HORIZON LINE.

3. You don't see we're here, on This Side, living our lives, because for you the Horizon Line is <u>always</u> <u>a day away</u>. You can walk for a thousand moons (or more for all I know), but you'll never reach it.

4. On the other paw, we know you're there because we visit you all the time. This is partly because of broomsticks. A broomstick has no trouble with any Horizon Line anywhere. A broomstick (with one or more of us upon it) just flies straight through.

And it has to be like that because scaring Otherside children into their wits is part of witches' work. In fact it is Number One on the Witches' Charter of Good Practice (see copy glued at the back).

On the other paw, it is NOWHERE in the Charter for a witch to go over to Your Side to make friends and try to be and do everything you are and do — <u>as my witch, Haggy Aggy, does.</u>

But then, that's my giant problem: being cat to a witch who doesn't want to be one. And as you will see from these diaries, it makes my life a right BAG OF HEDGEHOGS. So all I can say is, if HA tries to make friends with YOU, send her straight back to This Side with a spider in her ear.

Thank you,

Rumblewick Spellwacker Mortimer B. xxx

This Diary Belongs to:

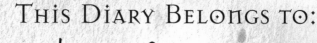

Rumblewick Spellwacker Mortimer B.

RUMBLEWICK for short, RB for shortest

Address:
Thirteen Chimneys,
Wizton-under-Wold, This Side
Bird's Eye View: 331 N by WW

Telephone:
77+3-5+1-7

Nearest Otherside Telephone:
Ditch and Candleberry Bush Street,
N by SE Over the Horizon

Birthday:
Windy Day 23rd Magogary

EDUCATION:
The Awethunder School for Familiars
12-Moon Apprenticeship to the
High Hag Witch Trixie Fiddlestick

QUALIFICATIONS:
Certified Witch's Familiar

CURRENT EMPLOYMENT:
Seven-year contract with Witch Hagatha Agatha,
Haggy Aggy for short, HA for shortest

HOBBIES:
Cathastics, Point-to-Point Shrewing, Languages

NEXT OF KIN:
Uncle Sherbet (retired Witch's Familiar)
Moldy Old Cottage,
Flying Teapot Street,
Prancetown

Nonstop Swan Lake Day Night

Dear Diary,

My Uncle Sherbet (now retired but once a famous Familiar) has been to visit.

I'd written to him many times about Haggy Aggy and her GIANT unwillingness to be a proper-practicing witch.

He always replied with good advice and helpful spells. Even so, I think he thought I was EXAGGERATING.

So I invited him to come and see for himself.

And guess what? She is just SO contra-turvy that for the three nights he was here, she behaved almost like a perfectly willing witch!!

She wore full witch's black (apart from a pink petticoat and a flower on her hat).

She hardly STOPPED crouping, crawing, and throat-hrobbling,

when she usually complains <u>cackling</u> is

cacophonous collywash!!

"Nothing like a good cackle-ophony to clear the air and send a message of witchradeship to your fellow Wiccans, don't you think, Sherbet?" she cawed when we went sightseeing over the Dragon's bog.

And when we
did go out, she
insisted on flying the broomstick
HERSELF — when mostly she claims
just looking at a broomstick makes her
feel broomstick-sick.

So now my favorite uncle has gone
home not suspecting but believing
I exaggerate her unwillingness.

But here's the thing, Diary.
I DO NOT.

In fact, if I tried for thirteen moons
I couldn't exaggerate it.

I mean, listen to this, the latest:

SHE IS ONLY PLANNING
TO BECOME
A BALLET DANCER.
Oh yes. No less.

And she is so serious about it, she's even
planning to begin where actual Otherside
ballet dancers
begin — at
ballet school

And yes, you may say YIKES on my behalf even if you don't know what ballet school is — because you soon will — and then you'll say TRIPLE YIKES.

This is how we arrived in this particular tricky sticky situation:

As soon as Sherbet left, she claimed to be completely witched-out — "helping you, RB, give your uncle a good impression of me." (Did I ask her to do that? No. The opposite. I wanted Sherbet to see her unwillingness to be a proper-practicing witch.)

Anyway, next she announced there was only one thing that could revive her:

an Otherside shopping spree.

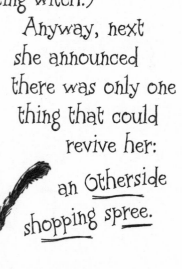

Flopping feebly into her room, she burst out soon after, brimming with spreefulness and wearing anything and everything

NOT BLACK.

She insisted we go in her pink car, not by broomstick. (At least it does have fly mode so we can get across the Horizon in it.)

As ever, once over there, she spent all she had left to spend on her Shopalot card — and then tried to spend more!! I got her away (before she was REFUSED and told to PUT THINGS BACK) by warning her that our car would soon be vanished by

Otherside Parking Guards if we didn't move it.

Then, as I was leading the way to the car, I turned and saw she wasn't with me.

She was staring transfixed into a shop window.

Going back, I saw the window was full of frothy skirts — some shaped like toadstool tops, some like white bluebells. There were feathery and gemmy things for wearing on the head. Shiny slipper shoes of white and pink, some with ribbons to crisscross up a leg.

And my witch was drooling.

"Oh, RB," she sighed.

"Such prettiness
    as dreams are made of.
We must go in and find out what
    all this is FOR!"
So we did — risking
    a vanished
        car.

Inside the shop there was a TV screen showing Othersiders dressed in the wear type that was in the window.

They were prancing, leaping, tripping, toetop-of-shoes-tipping, gliding, sliding, twirling, and sometimes SWOONING in each others' arms.

Watching, HA nearly SWOONED herself.

"What is it?" she screeched.

The shopping helper
screeched back (having no idea she
was talking to a witch, however unwilling),
"SWAN LAKE, of course, my dear!"

"Oh, oh, oh!" HA cried.
"How do I get to do Swan Lake?"

The shop clerk looked surprised but
answered softly, "Well, you'd start by going
to ballet school, I should think."

And that was that. Ballet school it was
and ballet school it is.

In a few tads of tell, HA got all the info
she needed from that willing shopping
helper. She found out where the nearest
ballet school is, its telephone number, and
how you get to go to it (apparently by
being so serious about becoming a Swan
Laker you won't take "no" for an answer).

Of course, when the shop clerk said
HA could buy a copy of the Swan
Lake film to watch at home,
she jumped at it. And because
she had no credit left
on her Shopalot,

THE
NUTCRACKER

SHE ORDERED ME TO LEAVE SOMETHING IN EXCHANGE!!

(Sadly, all I had was a foldaway broomstick, which I'd brought in case of a vanished car situation. So, it was goodbye to that finely tuned conveyance.)

Anyway, as a result — and in the interests of attending ballet school — she

has watched Swan Lake
NONSTOP,

from the moment we got home till she took it to bed with her, a short time ago.

And, worst luck, she made me watch it with her.

If I shut one eye for a split second, she jogged me with cries of,

"RB, wake up,
you can't
miss this bit!"

If I suggested making a cup of comfrey tea, she cried,

"No, no,
you can't miss
THIS bit!"

I now know <u>every</u> bit of that Swan Lake so well, I'm afraid to take a nap, even though I'm frazzled. Why? Because I know I'll be dancing it in my sleep.

Straight Hair, Phony Phone Call and the Hags Are On to Me Day Night

Dear Diary,

I was right to be afraid. Every moment I've been napping since I last wrote, I've been a dancing swan — and every moment I've been awake, I've been dancing around her and her dreams of ballet school!

Immediately after comfrey tea this morning, she ordered me to make her a Hair-Straightening Potion so she could flatten her wonderful witch's mop into a "beautiful ballet dancer's bun."

(Dead boring ballerina's bun, if you ask me.)

However, for your info,
here is my
Hair-Straightening
Recipe.

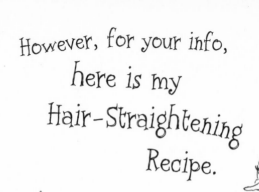

HAIR-STRAIGHTENING RECIPE

One pint swamp bilge
One pint frog spawn
Two ounces grated mildew
Two slugs, boiled,
cooled, and mashed
Sprinkling of dry rot
Teaspoon of wet rot

Mix ingredients together thoroughly until
there are no lumps and bind with rotten egg.
Leave to stiffen, then apply.

As I've told you, she has forbidden all live ingredients from our spells and potions.

So I tried to put her off using the Straightener by telling her about the slugs.

But all she said was, "Just this one time, RB, I will turn two blind eyes."

She was so eager, in fact, she used double quantities; and worst luck, her hair is now as flat as a flattened broomstick box.

Next, she sent me to the nearest Otherside library with a spell to make everyone present fall asleep while I found her a Ballet for Beginners book.

It was on my way back from that
exercise, when I met the High Hags.

They were clearly returning from an
all-night Children Scaring jaunt — because
they were in high spirits, singing, cackling,
bucking their broomsticks, AND NOT
LOOKING WHERE THEY WERE GOING.

Until they nearly collided with me.

Then they slowed down and started
pointing their pointing fingers.

Apparently they'd seen us the day
before — returning across the Horizon in
HA's pink car, HA dressed in anything and
everything NOT BLACK, and the car
overflowing with Otherside shopping.

"It is in your Contract of Service
to keep your witch in the ways of
proper practice," Dame Amuletta throbbled,
while the other three glared
as if they could see right through
to my bones.

"And proper-practicing witches wear black, use broomsticks, and prefer to shop on This Side at the Crafty Witches' Co-Op."

What could I say? She was
right on every count.

AND I KNEW IT!

"I try to do my best," was all
I could think of, stroking my Lucky
Whisker in the hope that the Ballet
for Beginners book wouldn't slip
out from under my hat.

"But sometimes . . ."
"Sometimes never!"

screeched Amuletta.

"Now, do better than your
best or you know what will happen."

And I do. They'll hang me over
a hot cauldron until my fur curls
and/or send me back to first
grade at the Awethunder
School for Familias.

As they flew away, all I could think was: I have to get HA off the whole idea of going to ballet school because if the High Hags get wind of THAT, I'm a curly-furred first grader for certain.

Only so far,
Dear Diary,
I am failing
giant
time.

As soon as I got home, HA grabbed the Beginners book, went to her room, and started speeding through it.

In what seemed like a few tads of tell, she came out claiming she'd "mastered" the "Five Basic Positions and a lot more" — and ordered me to fly her to the nearest Otherside telephone so she could call

the ballet

school!!

All I could think was SOCKS, SOCKS,
TADPOLES IN SOCKS.

Because if it's in my Contract of Service
to keep my witch in the ways of
proper practice, it's also in my contract
to obey her every whim and word.

What could I do? I flew her to that
see-through telephone booth on Ditch and
Candleberry Bush Street where — wait for it
— she made ME magic some Otherside money
out of the telephone's money box so she could
reuse it to call the ballet school!!

When I'd managed it — to some very strange stares from passing Othersiders — and she got to speak to someone,

she did so in the phoniest accent you've ever heard.

"I am a poor little hungry one from the f-f-f-frozen wastes of Sibericus," she simpered.

"Believe me, I haff never stopped being f-f-f-frozen, as you can hear. But in the interest of the great ballet, I haff stowed away on a trans-Siberican Sleigh to f-f-f-follow my dream of dancing the Swan Lake Swan Princess. Please giff me a chance. And don't make me take no for an answer. Please."

Well, the Othersiders at the ballet school must be out of their phony-sensing senses. They were completely taken in, and wait for it:

she's got herself
"a dance audition"
tomorrow — their
morning time of
10 o'clock!

Audition Day Night

Dear Diary,

"The audition" was a **nightsnake** and I had to live through every minute of it.

We crossed the Horizon by broomstick (the car wouldn't start, I made sure of that!). And then — on her insistence — we took an Otherside bus!! ("No one else will arrive by air, RB! And I don't want to look out of place on my first day.")

Immediately when we arrived, she disappeared into the "Girls' Room." When she came out I hardly recognized her.

She was barefoot, in a ragged torn-off dress with dirt rubbed into her face. (Apparently to make her look like a "poor little hungry thing" from the f-f-frozen wastes of wherever.)

Mind you, it worked.

The mad ballet school man and woman swooned.

"It's the Little Matchstick Girl!" they cried (whatever that is). "Now let's see what you can do."

Well, sad to relate, she could do everything because she'd not only studied that Ballet for Beginners book but — unbeknownst to me — she'd also done a ballet spell on herself.

Whatever they called out for her to do, she did perfectly. After the Five Basic Positions, they got really **excited**.

"Plié in first!" they called.

"Plié in second! Relevé! Relevé! Battement tendu! Rond de jambe, one, two, three! Very good, cherie!"

But it was her arabesque that did it. They flipped at her arabesque, all right.

Now my witch has a place at Otherside Ballet School, and if I don't keep this from the High Hags — I won't be OVER a hot cauldron, I'll be IN one till I'm back at the Awethunder School for Familiars —

a steamed cat dumpling.

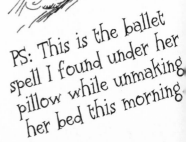

PS: This is the ballet spell I found under her pillow while unmaking her bed this morning

SPELL TO GET EVEN THE MOST LUMPEN BEING INTO BALLET SCHOOL

Your legs are now elastic and your
hips can turn right out
Your arms look smooth and boneless
as you spin and twirl about
Your body's strong and supple and can
leap into the air
There is no step you can't perform
and nothing you don't dare
First position, second position,
third position, four
Fifth position, feet turned out,
fully crossed, and more
The plié and the relevé, the splits,
the arabesque
And all of it from chanting this
while sitting at your desk.

(Repeat twelve times every day until
your audition is successful.)

The Hags Get Wind of It Day

Dear Diary,

SOCKS, SOCKS,

TADPOLES IN SOCKS!

The Hags <u>HAVE</u> got wind of

HA at ballet school!!

But let me go back a bit.

This morning when we arrived at the school, the Mad Two announced they are so pleased with HA's progress, they are going to create a special ballet for her for "the end of term show."

They were very excited, chucked her under her chin, and cried, "Oh, cherie, we think you are going to be a star! In fact, we are sure of it — you are going to be the next Pavlova!"

"Next Pavlova?"

HA almost screamed.

"How can I be a Pavlova?
From what I have seen in your
Eateries, this Pavlova is nothing
but a fluffguff, grubspit dessert!"

For some reason this made the Mad
Two laugh like tinkling bells and
chuck HA under the chin some
more.

"Oh no, cherie, the
dessert came much later!"
cried one of them. "Anna
Pavlova was one of the
greatest dancers the
world has ever
seen! Now,
come, let us
get to
work!"

Well, for me, these Pavlova
promises were so spirit-lowering,
I could not watch the warmup class
and sneaked home to do some chores.
I buried myself in untidying, invited
back all the eavesdroppers HA had
shooed out, and then went collecting
ingredients for our empty spell jars.
And that's where I bumped into the
High Hags, Trixie Fiddlestick and
Iodine Underwood.
AND FOUND OUT
THEY'D FOUND
OUT!

"Rumblewick
Spellwacker
Mortimer B,"

said Underwood. "How you do
disappoint us. It was only a yestermoment
that we warned you and now THIS!
Fiddlestick, tell him what you saw earlier."

So Fiddlestick told me. It was this: while flying past one of the ballet school windows, she'd seen HA, "twirling about in skintight nothing and unnatural stockings with a B.O.Y.— pronounced 'boy' — on the Other Side."

She was so boiling and bubbling, I could see there was no point in arguing. I could see they were thinking as they boiled and bubbled, "This Familiar's going to spend the rest of his life at Familiars' School if he doesn't come up with something good."

So I did. I came up with something brilliant, if I do say so myself. I said, "She is only in that ballet school to work on her child-scaring techniques."

Well, they seemed to believe me because they simmered right down but — and it's a GIANT but — in the morning they are coming to the school INVISIBLY to see HA's child-frightening work for themselves.

So between
now and then
I have to either:

1 convince HA to stop being
a Pavlova for a day and scare the other
ballet school children into their wits.

OR

2 if she refuses — which is likely, as
she already calls the children "her best
friends in the whole wide universe" — think
of a way of doing it myself.

Anyway, must dash as have
to collect HA and try to stop
her going for an after-class
"smoothie" with those new best
friends/want-to-be Pavlovas
of the non-dessert kind.

Bad Start for My Plan Day Night

Dear Diary,

While I was giving HA's aching feet a foot bath, I tried to introduce my plan. It was hard to get a word in edgeways.

"Tgghh . . ." she groaned.

"How they work me at that school. 'Lead with the heels, stretch the knees, direc' the toes, hold the turnout, lift the be-hind . . . bravo and again!' They work me so hard, I don't even have time to find a spell to turn me into a great ballerina overnight."

In the tad of breathtake that followed, I took my chance and said that maybe she wasn't meant to be a Pavlova. Maybe she should leave ballet school straight after class tomorrow. And before doing so, she should scare the other Pavlovas into their wits — as an act of reminding herself what she really is — a great witch when she is willing.

It was the wrong thing to say.

"Are you crazy?"

she screeched. "Scare the children? Leave ballet school? Tomorrow they will reveal the ballet they've created for me.

Tomorrow is the first day of the rest of my life!"

At this point I couldn't help myself. I blurted out that <u>tomorrow</u> the Hags would be in school, invisibly, to witness her child-scaring techniques, and if she didn't want me to be steamed, curly-furred, and back at Awethunder she'd better forget special ballets and start scaring.

Also the wrong thing to say.

She ranted she would NEVER frighten her new best friends in the whole wide universe. Not for me. Not for anything.

I pleaded but she dismissed my pleas. "Do something yourself, RB. STOP THOSE HAGS BEFORE THEY GET IN!"

Well, with all my talent and training, there's no way I can prevent High Hags from going anywhere INVISIBLY. So there's nothing else to do: I'll have to scare the children myself.

And as, in my experience, nothing scares those Otherside ratlets quite like big slimy toads . . . here goes.

I'm off to catch some — the bigger, the slimier, the better!

Slime Bun Award Fit and HA Storms a Convention Day — Well After Midnight

Dear Diary,

What a day, what a night! But I mustn't get ahead of myself.

I was telling you I was going toad-catching. And toad-catching I went. It was hard work, but by dawn I had a sack full of slimy GIANTS.

I lined them up and warned them of the brew they'd be in if they didn't help me out.

The biggest one only sneered. "Pull the other leg, RB. We all know you work for the famous Anti-Live Ingredientist Witch, Haggy Aggy, who has forbidden all living creatures from her potion-brewing."

"Only when
it suits her,"
I replied sternly.
"And if you won't do
what I ask, I'll hand you over
to my friend Grimey."
And that did the trick as
Grimey's witch has a BIG
reputation for toad-rich brews.
"All right," they croaked. "You win.
What do you want?"

I explained my
plan and to my
relief they agreed to
help — some even
with enthusiasm — as
they climbed back into
the sack, ready to be
flown to ballet school.

BUT — I then went to
get a broomstick, and as
I was returning, all I could hear
was HA frothing.

She'd stumbled over the sack! And, after
all my hard work collecting those toads,
she just emptied them over the fence
calling, "Hop away, my darlings!
Before that witch next door gets
her warty mitts on you!"

Now what,
I asked myself?
And decided

Dear Diary,

Sorry — fell asleep midsentence.

Where was I?
Oh yes,
trying to decide what to do
and coming up with precisely

NOTHING.

Nothing then — obviously, because I fell asleep — and nothing on the bus ride to school because HA kept interrupting my thoughts, babbling about starring in her own Special Ballet.

When we arrived, HA was just pulling on her leg warmers when the Mad Two called her aside.

"Cherie," they said, "The ballet we've created for you is ready. Today we start work. It is, of course,

THE LITTLE MATCH GIRL,

based on the famous fairy tale. You will dance the title role."

"Yes?" said HA eagerly.

"And what, I mean, vot, is the story?"

The Mad Two looked surprised, as if she should know it, but they told her anyway.

"It is the story of the poor little girl with no shoes who goes barefoot in the snow selling matches. She is so cold, she lights the matches to keep warm. In the light of each match she sees a wonderful vision. Finally she sees her dead grandmother, the only person who has ever loved her. In the morning, of course, she is frozen to death, but her soul is happy, soaring to heaven to that beloved grandmother.

And now, look . . . here is Madame Petrovsky, the wardrobe mistress."

Well, at that moment,
two things happened. First,
a window opened and in on the
breeze came the four High Hags.
They were invisible to everyone
else but, being in the know
and a well-trained Familiar,
I could see and hear
them perfectly.

They fluttered into some
chairs and fixed their eyes on
HA, waiting for her Scaring
of Children to start.

At the same time,
Madame Petrovsky was
holding up HA's raggedy
match girl costume.

At the sight of it HA went white, green, and puce. And my heart soared like the Little Match Girl's because WHITE-GREEN-PUCE IS THE SIGN THAT HA IS ABOUT TO THROW A PROPER WITCH'S FIT. And, as witch's fits go, this one took the Slime Bun Award.

She screeched, "Me? Dance in rags! Like that poor little nobody I came here as, from the frozen wastes of Sibericus? Not ever! I want beautiful feathers, a frothy,

frothy net! I want a glittery, starry princess tiara!"

She was so full of fit, she forgot not to be what she is — a witch — and rose into the air on a blast of fury.

As the Hags watched with obvious delight, HA shot bolts of white rage from her fingertips.

Of course, the little Pavlovas were terrified and ran for cover. But HA did not stop. Now she cast an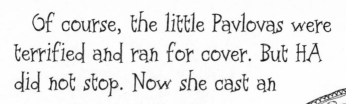

INANIMATE
OBJECTS
WALKABOUT
SPELL.

The costumes backstage slipped off
their rails and — like headless, legless
ghosts — characters from famous
ballets wafted around the hall.

Pieces of scenery came to life — painted
roses on a castle wall grew into a thorny
thicket. Gilded tables and chairs got up and
chased the little Pavlovas.

Mirrors flexed and reflected them back
       as fat little monsters
  till they screamed with horror.

The Hags were more than satisfied. They'd seen what they'd come to see, and now left the way they came — on the breeze.

Only High Hag Fiddlestick hung back to whisper, "Good work, RB. See you at the Witches' Convention tonight. I hope Haggy Aggy has prepared a good speech."

And, in that moment of otherwise triumph, all I could think was YIKES AND TRIPLE YIKES!!

I'd been so busy busing back and forth to ballet school, I'd forgotten all about the Convention.

Haggy Aggy didn't even have a SUBJECT for her speech, let alone written one word of it.

But then — call me good or what — I had a supernova idea.

It was obvious what the speech should be about, and the title came to me

in a flash:

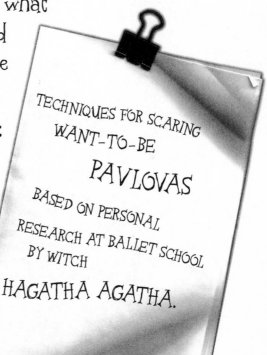

TECHNIQUES FOR SCARING WANT-TO-BE

PAVLOVAS

BASED ON PERSONAL RESEARCH AT BALLET SCHOOL BY WITCH

HAGATHA AGATHA.

Writing it wouldn't be a problem because I'd do that. Getting HA to deliver it, however, was quite another matter. But then I had my <u>super</u>, <u>supernova</u> idea — which I'll come to in a minute.

<u>First</u>, I went for the foldaway broomstick I'd hidden in HA's ballet bag. I flew up to HA and made her invisible using the Tried and Tested Out-of-Sighter every Familiar learns in first grade.

THE TRIED AND TRUSTED SPELL TO OUT-OF-SIGHT YOUR WITCH FOR HER OWN GOOD

Make a breeze by sneezing seven times.
Curl your Lucky Whisker backwards and chant:

It's in your own interest
That you're out of sight
So wherever you are
There is nothing but light,
Not an arm or a thumb
Not a leg or a tum
Not one scrap or one cell
Though you're perfectly well
Not a hair in between
When this spell is said
CAN BE SEEN!

Out of sight to everyone but me, I picked her up and then swooped under a frothy and feathered Swan Princess costume that was wafting about the hall.

In a few tads of trice, we were out of that ballet school, flying away through a window the Hags had thankfully left open — and heading for the safe haven of home!

Fortunately for my plan, being invisible does take the wind out of a witch's sails. So, as soon as we got back to Thirteen Chimneys, and I had reversed the Out-Of-Sighter, HA turned on the TV, lay on the sofa, and fell asleep.

All just as I hoped.

Because while she slept I wrote
her speech for the Convention.
And if I do say so myself,

it was something of

a masterpiece.

So now all I had to do was wake her and persuade her to go and deliver it!!!

It wasn't easy.

When I read her the title, she refused outright.

"But I love those children, RB. If I have scared them, it was by mistake. I didn't mean to. I didn't want to. It was just that I was so UPSET AND DISAPPOINTED by that horrid raggedy old dress they were going to make me wear. So, in a word,

NO!

I wouldn't give a speech like that even if I had to hang over a hot cauldron for the rest of my life!"

(Easy for her to say.)

But then — and here comes the **SUPER,**

SUPERNOVA IDEA

I mentioned earlier — I brought out the Swan Princess costume I'd had the good thinking to bring home.

By now, HA's spelling of it had worn off. It no longer had a life of its own. It was inanimate and ready to be stepped into.

I dangled it. Tempting her.

"Would you change your mind," I tempted,

"if you could get up on the stage wearing this?"

Well, ask a silly question!!

She lit up brighter than the
evening star — and
couldn't dress in
it or get to the

Convention
fast enough!

Of course, once there,
I still had one tricky sticky
problem to solve: explaining her
appearance to the High Hags.
As it turned out, I didn't have to.
They had been so impressed by what
they'd seen her do in the ballet school,

they "explained"

it to me!!

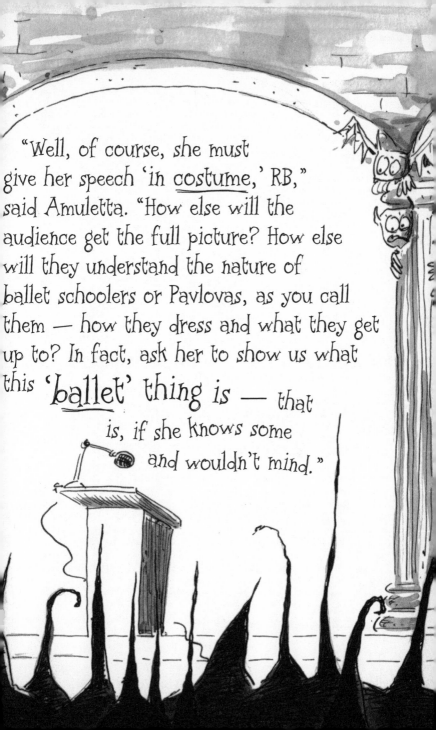

"Well, of course, she must give her speech 'in <u>costume</u>,' RB," said Amuletta. "How else will the audience get the full picture? How else will they understand the nature of ballet schoolers or Pavlovas, as you call them — how they dress and what they get up to? In fact, ask her to show us what this '<u>ballet</u>' thing is — that is, if she knows some and wouldn't mind."

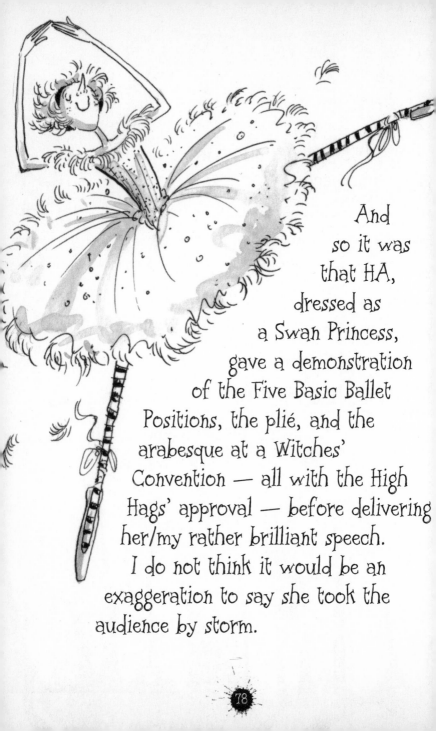

And
so it was
that HA,
dressed as
a Swan Princess,
gave a demonstration
of the Five Basic Ballet
Positions, the plié, and the
arabesque at a Witches'
Convention — all with the High
Hags' approval — before delivering
her/my rather brilliant speech.
I do not think it would be an
exaggeration to say she took the
audience by storm.

Even the Hags joined the standing ovation and had one of their toads present her with a huge bouquet of Poison Gallwort.

There was one disappointment, though. Uncle Sherbet had come to the Convention. He had been in the audience!! Afterward he came to congratulate me on the willingness of my witch "to forgo her black and her dignity for froth and frippery all in the interests of greater witchery."

I was so blue-mooned by this, I couldn't even say,

"OH, UNCLE SHERBET, IF ONLY YOU KNEW!"

Mind you, what is not disappointing one tad is that HA has now decided becoming a great ballet dancer is too much like hard work.

She says she's quite happy doing the odd arabesque in the Swan Princess costume, in front of the bathroom mirror.

Hopefully, she'll tire of that soon too.

And speaking of tiredness, I'm off for some proper Shut-Eye.

I'm so frazzled

I feel my fur falling out in handfuls.

But at least it's not curled —

NOT YET!

USEFUL EXPLANATIONS
ABOUT THINGS
YOU MAY NOT KNOW
AS YOU ARE A DIARY

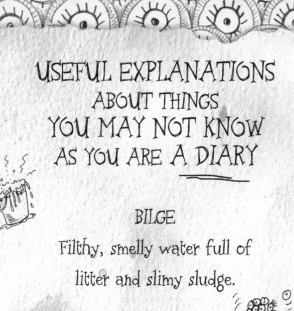

BILGE
Filthy, smelly water full of
litter and slimy sludge.

SPAWN
A teeming mass of eggs
(usually the work of frogs).

MILDEW
A teeming mass of mini mushrooms (fungi).

DRY ROT
Mini fungi that rot from the inside out.

WET ROT
Soggy mini fungi that
rot from the outside in.

CONTRACT OF SERVICE
What you've agreed to do for your
witch and what you'll get in return.

THE FIVE BASIC BALLET POSTIONS
The beginning and end of every ballet step, which
dancers must be able to do in their sleep.

PLIÉ (plee-AY)
Dance French for a bending of the knee or knees
with hips, legs, and feet turned straight
out (OUCH) and no falling over.

BATTEMENT TENDU (bat-MAHN tahn-DEW)
Dance French for sliding foot from
here to there without lifting your
toe from ground, both knees straight.
(Looks easy till you try it.)

ROND DE JAMBE (rawn duh jawmb)
Dance French for taking around the
legs — "EN TERRE" or "EN L'AIR" as the
Mad Ballet Two say, which means on
the ground or in the air.

CHERIE (sheh-RRIE)
Everyday French for "my dear."

ARABESQUE

Balancing on one leg with the other leg sticking out in a straight line behind you, EVERY BIT of it equal distance from the floor!!

PIROUETTE (peer-WET)

Dance French for a complete spin of the body on one foot without falling over. (KERWHISH!)

CONVENTION

A get-together of witches to exchange ideas on proper witches' practice and ever-greater witchery. Usually with speeches and clapping and extra-slimy slime buns afterward.

WITCHES' CHARTER
OF GOOD PRACTICE

I. Scare at least one child on the Other Side into his or her wits — every day (excellent), once in seven days (good), once a moon (average), once in two moons (bad), once in a blue moon (failed).

2. Identify any fully grown Othersiders who were not properly scared into their wits as children and DO IT NOW. (It is never too late for a grown Othersider to come to his or her senses.)

3. Invent a new spell useful for every purpose and every occasion in the Witches' Calendar. Ensure you or your Familiar commits it to a spell book before it is lost to the Realms of Forgetfulness forever.

4. Keep a proper witch's house at all times — filled with dust and spiders' webs, mold, and earwigs' underthings; and ensure the jars on your kitchen shelves are always alive with good spell ingredients.

5. Cackle a lot. Cackling can be heard far and wide and serves many purposes such as (i) alerting others to your terrifying presence and (ii) sounding hideous and thereby comforting to your fellow witches.

6. Make sure your Familiar keeps your means of proper travel (broomsticks) in good repair and that one, either, or both of you exercise them regularly.

7. Never fail to present yourself anywhere and everywhere in full witch's uniform (i.e., black everything and no ribbons upon your hat ever). Sleeping in uniform is recommended as a means of saving dressing time.

8. Keep your Familiar happy with a good supply of comfrey tea and slime buns. Remember, behind every great witch is a well-fed Familiar.

9. At all times acknowledge the authority of your local High Hags. As their eyes can move 360 degrees and they know everything there is to know, it is always in your interests to make their wishes your commands.

Dear Reader,

Haggy Aggy's made "bestest" best friends in the whole wide world with two very unwitchy girls. And they have asked her to sleep over tonight and she's said YES. Does that sound like witch behavior to you? I thought not. WHY ME?

Pick-up my next diary, <u>My Unwilling Witch Sleeps Over</u>, to find out why I'm going totally bats on a broomstick.

Sincerely,

Rumblewick
Spellwacker Mortimer B.

Dear Diary,

We're home, thank the stars. Back from the Far Quagmires, though by no means out of the "quagmire."

To continue: what with the grubspit feelings of guilt and having to sleep over—by the time the fog lifted and we came to leave Pondernot's—HA's mood was so dark she could hardly see her way out of the front door.

Though I was standing there ready with our broomstick, she walked straight past me and nearly fell into one of the bog fires in what Pondernot fondly calls her

"garden."

This put her into
an even fouler mood.
Followed by an even fouler one,
when Pondernot said with a crooked
smile, "Now my dear, you know how
much it would upset me to see
a fully-fledged witch being flown by
her Familiar. So I hope you'll be flying
that broomstick home yourself as any
AUNT-RESPECTING witch would do."
With a thundery snarl, HA grabbed
our broomstick, mounted it, and
took off with barely time for
me to leap on behind.

Well, the truth is, Diary, in the dark
mood she was in, HA should NOT have been
flying anything, anywhere. Let alone from
the Far Quagmires to Wizton-Under-Wold.
It requires much alertness of the stars above
and landmarks below. It should NEVER be
attempted by one in a personal eclipse and
hardly able to see

her own flying hand
            in front of her.

So, inevitably, in spite of my attempts to navigate from the back of the broom,

WE WENT THE <u>WRONG WAY</u>.

We went so wrong, we ended up crossing the Horizon and flying uselessly hither and thither on the Other Side, until HA said she was feeling so sick she was going to fall off.

I took my life in my paws, clung and clawed my way past her to take over the flying, and quickly brought us down—as I thought safely—on

the nearest suitable landing place.

As it turned out—it wasn't safe
or suitable.

It was the roof of a building in which,
HA was soon to discover, Otherside
children go to do JIM (similar to
catnastics, if a clumsier version).

And now that we were off-broomstick
and away from guilt and the Far
Quagmires, HA's dark

mood
suddenly
lifted.

Her sun and moon came out again.

She dangled cheerfully from the water pipes of the building, so she could peer in and eavesdrop at a half-open window.

"Oh RB," she cried, "do take a look.

"There are darling girls in there doing what they call JIM—leaping, tumbling, propelling, and turning free through the air. No springs on their feet, no wings on their shoulders! Oh, how I'd love to be what they are and do what they do. And do you know what? Because I would love to, I've decided _I will!_"

Well, you know
Haggy Aggy.
Once she's
decided, she's decided.
So forget Pondernot's
guiltifyings about being more
Other Side than This Side.

An Otherside JIM girl
is what HA
is going to be!!

Dear Precious Children,

The Publisher asked me to say something about these Diaries.
(As I do not write Otherside very well, I have dictated it to
the Publisher's Familiar/assistant. If she has not written it
down right, let me know and I'll turn her into a fat pumpkin.)

This is my message: I went to a lot of trouble to steal these
Diaries for you. And the Publisher gave me a lot of shoes in
exchange. If you do not read them the Publisher may want the
shoes back. So please, for my sake — the only witch in
witchdom who isn't willing to scare you for her own
entertainment — ENJOY THEM BOTH.
Yours ever,

Haggy Aggy

Your fantabulous shoe-loving friend,
Hagatha Agatha (Haggy Aggy for short, HA for shortest) xx

Hello, this is the Publisher's Familiar here. After the publication of these diaries, Rumblewick Spellwacker Mortimer B. naturally became an international phenomenon, renowned for his wit, wisdom, and knack for tackling tricky, sticky situations. This very busy cat sat down for an interview with Yours Truly and spilled the beans on favorite spells, Catnastics, and that most unwilling witch, Haggy Aggy.

PUBLISHER'S FAMILIAR: You've become immensely popular on the Other Side because of these diaries. Tell me, are you a star on Your Side as well?

RUMBLEWICK: In my eyes, I am a megalight of marvelwockery on ALL sides. And as any wisewit knows it is not how others see you but how one sees oneself that counts. But, no. Apart from my best friend, Grimey, who fully appreciates my cat-abilities, I am not star-spangled on Our Side. Worst luck. In fact I think some of the other Familiars may even feel sorry for me. SOCKS, SOCKS, and triple yikes. On the other hand, HA's burning ambitions to become galaxy-sized in the wider world of non-witches are simmering far too successfully for my liking. She will probably explode like a shooting star all over Otherside Celebrity-ness very soon.

PF: Is HA your first witch since your graduation from the Awethunder School for Familiars?

RB: HA is the ONLY witch I've been in service to apart from my seven-moon apprenticeship to the High Hag Fiddlestick, which was like puffing dandelions compared to working for HA.

And, of course I'd rather assist a proper witch like Grimey's, Witch Understairs. Even so, I'd say every Familiar should be exposed to the helter-skelter of an unwilling witch at some point, and tested on the Scariest Rides of Life.

PF: With her love of pink and fondness for Otherside activities, Haggy Aggy can no doubt be a most frustrating witch. But despite her antics, you do seem to be quite fond of her. What do you like best about HA?

RB: She is my witch and I am her cat. I would fly to the ends of the next galaxy for her and be back in time for comfrey tea and slime buns. Besides, I know that underneath all that pink froth and frip-trippery, there's a seriously supernova witch glowing with ideas from the Dark Ages who couldn't live without me and who is going to wake up one lunchtime soon and remember to shine on THIS SIDE!

PF: You list Catnastics as one of your hobbies. What does it involve?

RB: I was always good at Catnastics in school because I have a head for heights, probably thanks to my Lucky Whisker that knows balance backward. It mainly involves turning continuous triple body spins as you fly through the air without the assistance of magic before landing softly upon all fours. And it's not as easy as it sounds, believe me.

PF: What was your favorite class at the Awethunder School for Familiars, and what was the most useful spell you learned while there?

RB: I loved all my classes at Awethunder, but the one that nudged to the top of my thrill-list was Practical Disguise. I had the gift. I could think myself into a disguise in a tad of tell. Once I disguised our teacher as a disguised disguise so triple presto she didn't even know she had been disguised. I won the Class Prize for that. And given my current situation, one of the most useful things I learned in Spelling was the tried and trusted "Keep Your Witch Upright" spell.

PF: What advice do you have for ballerinas, Familiars, and writers-in-training?

RB: My advice for wannabe Otherside ballerinas is: (1) Learn the Five Basic Ballet Positions without using magic, which is cheating. (2) Say "cherie" a lot and speak with that funny accent called French, and most importantly, (3) before you start a ballet class, check that there isn't a witch at the barre, pretending she isn't one. My advice to Familiars is: think and spell on your paws, keep out of the Abyss of Trouble, avoid the Narrow Avoid, and don't let the High Hags hang you over a hot cauldron till your fur curls. And if your witch disappoints, don't get down, get inventive. As for my advice to writers-in-training: if you're writing a diary, keep it under lock and key so it cannot be stolen from your log basket and sold to a publisher for a lifetime supply of shoes, as happened to me . . . and write from the heart, though don't be afraid to sprinkle well with Imagination Dust.

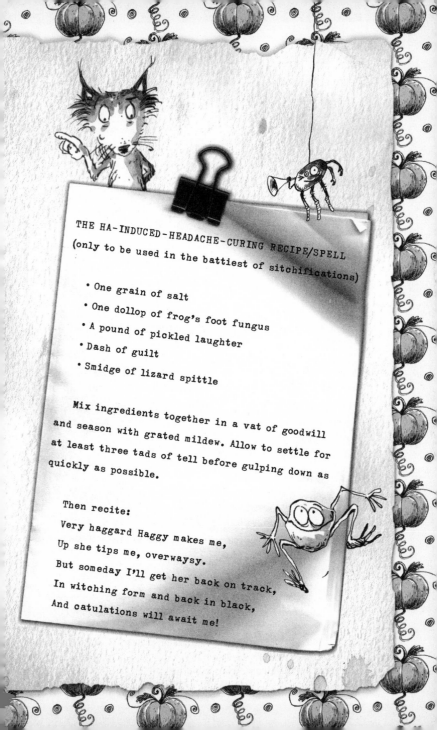

THE HA-INDUCED-HEADACHE-CURING RECIPE/SPELL
(only to be used in the battiest of sitchifications)

- One grain of salt
- One dollop of frog's foot fungus
- A pound of pickled laughter
- Dash of guilt
- Smidge of lizard spittle

Mix ingredients together in a vat of goodwill and season with grated mildew. Allow to settle for at least three tads of tell before gulping down as quickly as possible.

Then recite:
Very haggard Haggy makes me,
Up she tips me, overwaysy.
But someday I'll get her back on track,
In witching form and back in black,
And catulations will await me!